3 1994 00938 0053

3/00

SANTA ANA PUBLIC LIBRARY
NEWHOPE BRANCH

I062412E

Turtle Songs
A Tale for
Mothers and Daughters

Written by Margaret Olivia Wolfson
Illustrated by Karla Sachi

BEYOND
WORDS
Publishing

J 398.20996 WOL
Wolfson, Margaret
Turtle songs

$15.95
NEWHOPE   31994009380053

Beyond Words Publishing, Inc.
20827 N.W. Cornell Road, Suite 500
Hillsboro, Oregon 97124-9808
503-531-8700 / 1-800-284-9673
www.beyondword.com

Text copyright © 1999 by Margaret Olivia Wolfson
Illustrations copyright © 1999 by Karla Sachi

All rights reserved. No part of this book may be reproduced or transmitted in any form or
by any means, electronic or mechanical, including photocopying, recording, or by any
information storage and retrieval system, without the written permission of
Beyond Words Publishing, Inc., except where permitted by law.

Edited by Marianne Monson-Burton
Designed by Beth Hansen-Winter

Distributed to the book trade by Publishers Group West
Printed in Singapore

Library of Congress Cataloging-in-Publication Data

Wolfson, Margaret Olivia, 1953-
     Turtle songs : a tale for mothers and daughters / written by
Margaret Olivia Wolfson ; illustrated by Karla Sachi.
          p.   cm.
     Summary : When he hears their plaintive songs, the sea god turns Rani
and her mother into sea turtles to keep them from being kidnapped.
     ISBN 1-885223-95-1 (cloth)
     [1. Folklore—Fiji.]   I. Sachi, Karla, ill.   II. Title.
PZ8.1.W835Tu 1999
[398.2'099611'01]—dc21   98-41583
                                                                          CIP
                                                                          AC

The corporate mission statement of Beyond Words Publishing, Inc.: *Inspire to Integrity*

To my dear mother, Esther, and to the following mothers and daughters
who all alone have braved life's rugged seas:

Mim and Beret

Meg and Katherine

Isha and Maya

Marlene and Margaretha

—Margaret—

For Aaron, who plays with angel turtles, and for Randy,
who pulled out my hidden paintings

—Karla—

Long ago on the little island of Kadavu, a Princess lived with her daughter. The Princess and her daughter were both very beautiful. Their cocoa-colored skin was smooth, and clusters of golden cowrie shells gleamed around their necks.

One day the Princess said, "Daughter, let's go to the far reef and catch some fish."

Oh, yes, I'd like that!" said the little girl, whose name was Rani.

So they piled up their canoe with nets and ropes and baskets and paddled through the green and glassy sea until they reached their destination.

By noon their baskets brimmed with fish. Smiling, the Princess and Rani lowered their catch into the boat.

Afterward, they sat side by side on the beach and watched the glittering waves tumble, one after another, to shore.

Because the sea was so beautiful, the Princess longed to be part of it forever. She imagined three turtles paddling up a path of sun-bubbled water, a school of rainbow fish sparkling in their wake.

She turned to her daughter and said, "Sometimes I wish we were a pair of giant turtles."

"Me too!" Rani said, her eyes brightening. "Then we could swim all day long!" Rani ran to the water's edge. She waved her arms back and forth, pretending to be a turtle. The Princess smiled, delighted to see her daughter so cheerful. Rani's father had been swept out to sea many years ago, and since that time, Rani had often been sad. Feeling a little sleepy, the Princess slipped into a daydream.

The Princess pushed against her beached canoe. The boat creaked noisily but barely moved. She pushed again. To her relief, the sand released its grip and the canoe slipped into the water. "Hurry, Rani! Get in!" she shouted.

The Princess began rowing. But even though she was an expert oarswoman, she was no match for the two men.

"Stop!" they bellowed. "Stop!"

"Mother, I'm scared!" Rani whimpered as she huddled at the bottom of the canoe. The Princess pulled harder on the oars but made no reply.

The men slammed their canoe against the Princess's craft. As the short man steadied the boat, the tall man, his arms dripping with vines, climbed aboard. Using the vines as ropes, he began binding the Princess and Rani.

"Let us go!" the Princess demanded as she struggled to free herself. Her captor only laughed and drew the vines tighter. "You're coming with us," he snarled. "We need more people on our island."

"You won't get away with this!" the Princess snapped as he hoisted them into his boat. "Our villagers will rescue us!"

In answer, the short man stretched out his oar and capsized her canoe. Next, he yanked off the Princess's necklace and tossed it into the sea. For a moment, the golden shells bobbed up and down and then they slowly sank from sight. "When your boat and necklace wash ashore, your people will think you've drowned," he said. His lips curved into a nasty smile. "No one will come to look for you."

The Princess fell silent, knowing he spoke the truth. All the people in the village knew about the deadly currents that coursed beneath the sea's calm surface.

"Mother, what are we going to do?" Rani sobbed. For several moments the Princess remained silent, her brow puckered in thought. But then softly she began to sing. Long ago her grandmother had taught her that the sea god could be summoned through the magical power of song. Soon Rani joined in.

"Stop singing!" the short man demanded.

"Oh, let them sing," the other one said. "It's better than listening to them wail."

So as the two men rowed, the Princess and Rani sang. They sang and sang, only stopping when thunder rumbled on the horizon.

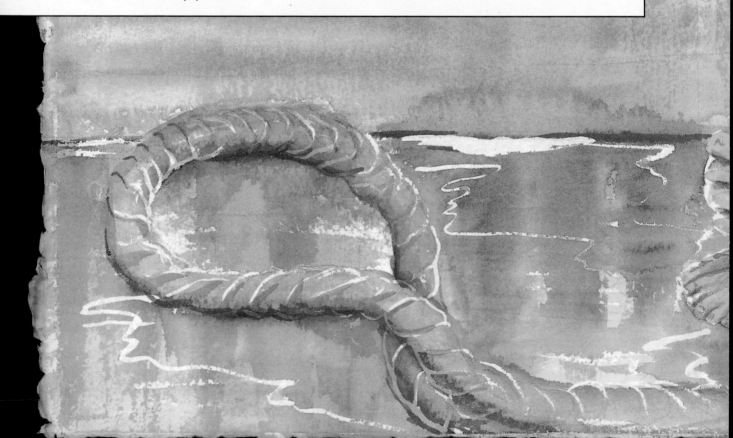

Soon a fierce wind arose and icy rains sliced the clouds.

"Don't be afraid!" the Princess cried as the waves battered the sides of the boat and swirled over its top. "Be brave, my daughter! The sea god will save us!"

As soon as she spoke, a thunderbolt cracked in the sky and a giant wave heaved the little canoe high into the air. For a second, the boat hovered on the wave's back. But when the giant swell rolled forward, the canoe plunged through the air, tossing the Princess, Rani, and the men overboard.

Screaming, they struck the water. But at that same moment —a miracle! Through some unseen magic, the Princess and Rani were changed into giant sea turtles! With their powerful flippers, they burst free from their prison of vines and began swimming toward Kadavu.

By the time they arrived, the storm had ended. The sun, slowly
sinking below the horizon, rippled the sea with nets of gold.
Dozens of girls and women stood on the shore, calling out to
the sea god—begging him to return their beloved Princess and Rani. One
woman sobbed as she pressed the Princess's shell necklace close to her
heart.

All of a sudden, a small girl tugged at her mother's arm. "Look!" she

shouted, "Out on the water! Something is moving!" The women followed the girl's gesture. Not far off they spotted two turtles. Before long, the two turtles were floating in the tides. Their shells, steeped in the golden waters, gleamed softly.

The women and girls waded out and crowded around the magnificent creatures. For a few moments there was silence. Then, to everyone's astonishment, the largest turtle spoke:

"I am your Princess, and the small turtle is my daughter. Today two bad men tried to kidnap us, but the sea god heard our cries and rescued us. In gratitude, we will swim his waters forever. But don't be sad. We have often longed to be part of the sea, and now our wish has come true. And though we will no longer live among you, we won't forget you. Whenever you want to see us, stand near the water and sing. I promise we will come."

"Yes, we will come!" Rani echoed.

Then, as the sun's last rays fanned across the sky,
the Princess taught the women many beautiful songs.
When she finished, she began paddling out to sea with Rani
following close behind. The women and girls called out their blessings.
Some tossed garlands on the water.

Ever since that time, the women and girls of Kadavu have called out to the Princess and her daughter. Hearing their songs, the two turtles—sometimes alone, sometimes with another large turtle—swim up from the depths.

Seeing them, the singers feel happy. They know that if they remember the turtles—and the turtles remember them—all will be well with the world.

AUTHOR'S NOTE: For many of the world's peoples, song has long provided a way of communicating with the ancestral spirits and the forces of nature. In the village of Namuana, on the Fijian island of Kadavu (also spelled Kandavu), women still follow the age-old custom of singing to the turtles. Hearing their voices, the turtles swim up from the depths. When the singers see the turtles, they know that the *vu*—the ancestral spirits—are showing their love and, because of this, harmony will prevail in the world.

To this day, in honor of the Turtle Princess and her daughter, the villagers of Kadavu do not eat turtle meat, despite the fact that it is prized throughout the region.

My version of this story blends two variations of this ancient myth; however, it most closely corresponds to the version as related by the villagers of Namuana. And though I have added many details for artistic purposes and have fleshed out the myth's plot line and characters, *Turtle Songs* remains true to its traditional sources. My story was largely inspired by two accounts of the myth as collected by Nadine Amadio in Fiji and published in her book *Pacifica: Myth, Magic and Traditional Wisdom from the South Sea Islands*.

Depending on the source, the spelling of the Princess's and the daughter's names varies. The Turtle Princess's name is spelled as either Tinaicaboga or Tinandi Thambonga. Her daughter (which for the ease of young readers I have shortened to Rani) can appear as either Raunindalithe or Raudalice.

I believe this myth and its accompanying ritual remind us of our deep and abiding bond with the natural world, particularly with the oceans and the creatures that swim its waters. It also movingly expresses the powerful link between mother and daughter.

ARTIST'S NOTE: For centuries, Fiji has been a crossroads and a meeting place for the Melanesian and Polynesian peoples, which I have tried to reflect in the artwork.

I have incorporated many traditional details that suggest the heroines' royal status. For instance, the white cowrie shell was worn only by royalty and often adorned the huts of chiefs. Power was also believed to be in the hair, and to have an abundance of hair was the sign of a regal person.

The women are dressed in tapa cloth, which is made in Fiji by stripping bark from the paper mulberry tree. This bark is pounded with a mallet on a log until it becomes very soft, and patterns are painted onto the cloth in shades of brown and black.